A NOTE TO PARENTS

When your children are ready to "step into reading," giving them the right books is as crucial as giving them the right food to eat. **Step into Reading Books** present exciting stories and information reinforced with lively, colorful illustrations that make learning to read fun, satisfying, and worthwhile. They are priced so that acquiring an entire library of them is affordable. And they are beginning readers with a difference—they're written on five levels.

Early Step into Reading Books are designed for brand-new readers, with large type and only one or two lines of very simple text per page. **Step 1 Books** feature the same easy-to-read type as the Early Step into Reading Books, but with more words per page. **Step 2 Books** are both longer and slightly more difficult, while **Step 3 Books** introduce readers to paragraphs and fully developed plot lines. **Step 4 Books** offer exciting nonfiction for the increasingly independent reader.

The grade levels assigned to the five steps—preschool through kindergarten for the Early Books, preschool through grade 1 for Step 1, grades 1 through 3 for Step 2, grades 2 through 3 for Step 3, and grades 2 through 4 for Step 4—are intended only as guides. Some children move through all five steps very rapidly; others climb the steps over a period of several years. Either way, these books will help your child "step into reading" in style!

Library of Congress Cataloging-in-Publication Data
Hayes, Geoffrey.
The night of the circus monsters / by Geoffrey Hayes. p. cm. — (Step into reading. A step 3 book)
SUMMARY: Ducky Doodle loves sea monsters so much that he fails to recognize a crook when Doctor Ocular's Sea Monster Circus comes to Boogle Bay.
ISBN 0-679-87113-6 (pbk.) — ISBN 0-679-97113-0 (lib. bdg.)
[1. Animals—Fiction. 2. Sea monsters—Fiction.] I. Title. II. Series: Step into reading.
 Step 3 book. PZ7.H31455Ni 1995 [Fic]—dc20 94-43103

Manufactured in the United States of America 10 9 8 7 6 5 4 3 2 1

Random House, Inc. New York, Toronto, London, Sydney, Auckland

STEP INTO READING is a trademark of Random House, Inc.

Step into Reading

THE NIGHT OF THE CIRCUS MONSTERS

BY GEOFFREY HAYES

WITH AN ALL-STAR CAST!

HAS TO BE SEEN TO BE BELIEVED!

A Step 3 Book

Random House New York

There was a new poster on the Boogle Bay dock. Otto, Olivia, and Ducky Doodle gathered around to read it.

> Amazing Circus
> With Rare Sea Monsters!
> Feats of Magic!
> One Night Only!

4

"Wow! I want to go!" cried Ducky Doodle.

"There are no such things as sea monsters," said Olivia.

"That's not true," said Otto. "Uncle Tooth told me he met one once."

"And you believed him?" said Olivia.

"Of course," said Otto. "I believe everything Uncle Tooth tells me."

Uncle Tooth was sitting on the pier mending fishnets. Otto, Olivia, and Ducky Doodle ran over to ask him.

"Ah, yes," answered Uncle Tooth. "That happened in my youth. A giant sea lizard was destroying ships and eating their cargoes of food. He liked every kind of food. But his favorite treat was mandarin oranges. I had the clever idea of painting a bunch of cannonballs to look like oranges. I tricked him into eating them."

"Then what happened?" asked Ducky Doodle.

"The cannonballs were so heavy that he sank to the bottom of the sea. He hasn't been heard from since."

"Poor monster," said Doodle.

"Is that a true story, or are you making it up?" asked Olivia.

"I'll leave it to you to decide," said Uncle Tooth.

"I saw a sea monster off Crabshell Cove," said Ducky Doodle. "I was going to feed it some jellybeans, but it swam away."

Otto and Olivia burst out laughing.

"You're just trying to be like Uncle Tooth," said Otto.

"I am not!" yelled Ducky Doodle.

"If Ducky Doodle says he saw a sea monster, I believe him," said Uncle Tooth.

Just then, Ducky Doodle saw something else. Auntie Hick was coming along the street. He hid behind Uncle Tooth. "She's angry because I forgot to finish my chores," he said.

"Forgot? Or didn't want to?" whispered Uncle Tooth.

Auntie Hick came over. She pulled Doodle out from behind Uncle Tooth.

"Um…Uncle Tooth was just telling us some stories," Doodle stammered.

"Stuff and nonsense!" snorted Auntie Hick.

"Exactly what *I* said," agreed Olivia.

Auntie Hick squinted at her.

"Don't you have homework to do, young lady?"

Auntie Hick grabbed Olivia with one hand and Ducky Doodle with the other.

"You should be ashamed of yourself," she told Uncle Tooth. "Filling these kids' heads with fairy tales when they have chores and homework to do!"

Then she marched Olivia and Doodle home, complaining all the way.

As soon as his chores were done, Ducky Doodle grabbed his spyglass and ran down to the beach.

Dark clouds rolled in. The air was chilly. A wind had come up. Was that a sea monster's tail? Or just the crest of a wave?

Ducky Doodle wandered over to Crabshell Cove. He was surprised to see an odd-looking vessel bobbing in the water. Behind it was a string of empty cages. On the beach were the weasel twins, Jiminy and Biminy. They were painting a large sign:

When they saw Doodle watching them,
they ran over and snatched the spyglass
from his hand.

"Spying, were you?" said Jiminy.

"We don't like spies," said Biminy.

Doodle reached for his spyglass.

"Give that back!" he cried. "I need it to
hunt for sea monsters!"

"Did someone say 'sea monsters'?" asked a deep voice.

A large gentleman smoking a cigar stood on the deck of the floating vessel. He came down a gangway and told Jiminy and Biminy to let Ducky Doodle go.

"I wasn't spying," Doodle said.

"Of course you weren't," said the gentleman. "It's an honor to meet you, Mr…"

"Doodle. Ducky Doodle. My pa was Blackeye Doodle, the pirate."

"Ah, yes, Blackeye, I know that name," said the gentleman. "By the way, my name is Doctor Ocular. If you are hunting for sea monsters, perhaps I can help you. What say we go into my Floating Laboratory?"

"Are…are the sea monsters in there?" asked Ducky Doodle nervously.

"Oh, my, no," said Doctor Ocular.

He led Ducky Doodle up the gangway.
"They are asleep in those caves at the end
of the beach. I will put them in the cages
tomorrow."

They boarded the dark vessel. It was littered with fabric, paints, brushes—even an air pump.

"Are the monsters real?" Ducky Doodle asked.

"Of course they are. It took me years to capture them all."

"Won't they be cramped in those cages?"

"Not at all," replied Doctor Ocular. "Sea monsters don't have feelings."

"What do you feed them?"

"Oh, just leftovers. That reminds me: You seem like an adventurous young man. I am looking for just such a person to be my assistant."

Doodle's face lit up. "Really?"

"Yes. If you help me by handing out fliers, I'll let you feed my monsters—whatever food you like."

"Oh, boy! Deal!" cried Ducky Doodle.

He took a handful of fliers.

"I'll do a real good job…honest!"

He hurried off the Floating Laboratory. When he reached Jiminy and Biminy, they moved to block his path.

"Tut-tut!" called the doctor. "Mr. Doodle is doing some important work for me."

They let him through.

"That's right—move it," said Doodle. "I have to hurry so I can feed the sea monsters."

"That should be some trick!" snickered the twins as Doodle ran off.

Doctor Ocular laughed, too. "He'll be so busy he won't have time to spy on us," he said.

Ducky Doodle ran back to town. Soon he'd be onstage, feeding the monsters in front of everybody!

First, he stopped at Auntie Hick's shop. "Do you have any mandarin oranges?" he asked.

"I thought you only liked pizza."

"Oh, they aren't for me. I'm going to feed them to the sea monsters," said Doodle.

He handed Auntie Hick a flier.

"This is the last straw," she huffed. "You know what I think of circuses and sideshows!"

Ducky Doodle didn't, but he could guess.

"Please!" he begged.

"Oh, all right," said Auntie Hick. "But you must pay for them out of your allowance."

"Thank you, Auntie Hick!" cried Ducky Doodle.

Just then, Uncle Tooth came in with Otto and Olivia.

"I'm going to feed the monsters," Doodle told them. "Doctor What's-his-name told me so." He gave them fliers, too.

"Who?" asked Olivia.

"Doctor Ocu-something. He's their owner."

"That name sounds familiar," said Otto. "But it's funny. His name isn't on the flier."

"I'll bet money it's a fake," said Olivia.

"It's not a fake!" yelled Doodle. "Uncle Tooth said sea monsters are real."

"That I did," said Uncle Tooth. "But don't take my word for it. You must see for yourself."

Ducky Doodle wasn't listening.

"I'll show you all!" he shouted as he raced out the door.

Ducky Doodle spent the afternoon
handing out fliers and inviting people to
the show. That night, when he went to bed,
he dreamed of sea monsters.

The next morning, Ducky Doodle found a circus tent on the docks.

Not far off was the Floating Laboratory. But where were the cages? "They must be in the tent," thought Doodle. That meant the monsters must be in there, too.

Ducky Doodle felt a shiver of fear. Then he ran off to hand out the rest of his fliers.

Otto and Olivia found the tent next.

"It must have been put up during the night. Very mysterious!" said Otto.

"Crooked, if you ask me," said Olivia.

They smelled cigar smoke. The curtains parted and Doctor Ocular appeared.

"Good morning, kiddies," he said. "Don't miss the show tonight. Get your parents to bring you."

Otto jumped back. He knew that man! "That's Doctor Ocular," he whispered to Olivia. "He's a crook!"

"I could have told you that," she said.

"No. I mean it. He once tried to shipwreck Uncle Tooth and me! You keep an eye on him. I'm going to warn Uncle Tooth."

"Will do," said Olivia.

Otto dashed off.

When Doctor Ocular went back into the tent, Olivia tiptoed over to it and lifted a flap.

No one was watching, so she slipped inside.

Doctor Ocular and the weasel twins

were standing near some large cages. Were monsters in them? Olivia couldn't tell.

"Once everyone is inside the tent," said the doctor, "I will start the show. Then you two can move through the crowd picking pockets. Got that?"

"Loud and clear," said Jiminy. "And once the show is over, we get away in your Floating Laboratory."

Just then, his sharp eyes spotted Olivia.

He grabbed her before she could escape.

"I didn't hear anything, you crooks!" shouted Olivia.

"We can't take that chance," said Doctor Ocular.

They tied Olivia's hands, gagged her, and put her in an empty cage.

"A minor setback," Doctor Ocular told the weasels. "Come. The crowd will be arriving soon."

Otto found Uncle Tooth at the police station. He and Captain Poopdeck were playing checkers.

"I thought there was something fishy about that circus," said Uncle Tooth. "But we can't arrest Doctor Ocular. He hasn't done anything yet."

"What *can* we do?" asked Otto.

"Keep an eye on him," said Uncle Tooth.

"Olivia is doing that right now," said Otto.

Uncle Tooth took a thoughtful puff on his pipe. "Hmmm…knowing Olivia, I hope that's all she's doing."

By evening, there was quite a crowd in front of the circus tent.

"It looks like everyone in Boogle Bay is here," said Uncle Tooth.

"Everyone except Olivia," said Otto. "I've been searching for her all afternoon."

"And Ducky Doodle," said Auntie Hick. "I've been searching for him all afternoon. I've said time and time again that these circuses are bad for children."

"Oh, quit your yapping and help us look," said Uncle Tooth. "They could be in danger!"

"Well, I never!" said Auntie Hick.

Doctor Ocular opened the ticket booth. The crowd lined up. In no time, every last ticket had been sold.

Doctor Ocular's pockets were bulging with cash.

Just as he was putting the money in his carpetbag, Ducky Doodle showed up. He had a bag, too. His bag was filled with mandarin oranges.

"I've handed out all the fliers, Doctor Ocular," he said.

"Good boy."

"When can I feed the monsters?"

"Later," said Doctor Ocular. "Now out of my way. I have a show to put on."

Ducky Doodle started to follow Doctor Ocular into the tent, but Jiminy and Biminy blocked his path.

"Where's your ticket?" they asked.

"I don't need a ticket," said Doodle. "I'm Doctor Ocular's assistant."

"No ticket, no show," called Doctor Ocular as he walked off.

The weasel twins closed the tent flap in Ducky Doodle's face.

Otto and Uncle Tooth had tickets. They were inside with the crowd. But they still could not find Olivia.

Some scratchy music came on over the loudspeaker, and the houselights dimmed. Doctor Ocular appeared onstage.

He gave a long speech about his skill in taming sea monsters.

Just as the audience was getting bored, he held up an eyeball in a jar.

Everyone gasped in horror.

"I know an olive when I see one," Auntie Hick whispered to Uncle Tooth.

Next, the doctor did some card tricks.

Otto noticed Jimmy and Biminy moving through the crowd.

"Watch them," he told Uncle Tooth. "I'm going to look for Olivia."

Otto slipped outside. He heard someone crying round back. It was Ducky Doodle.

"Doodle!" he cried. "I was worried about you. Why aren't you inside?"

Ducky Doodle told Otto about Doctor Ocular.

"That man is up to no good," said Otto. "But we need evidence."

He crawled inside the tent, and Ducky Doodle followed, carrying his bag of oranges. "Maybe I can feed the monsters back here," he thought.

It was dark backstage. Behind the curtain were several cages with creatures in them. They wiggled about and stared at Doodle with strange, wide eyes. He backed away.

One of the creatures began shaking its cage and making angry noises.

"I'm scared," said Doodle.

"Me, too," said Otto.

Ducky Doodle noticed that the monster making all the noise was smaller than the others. It didn't look scary. In fact, it looked like…

"Olivia!" cried Ducky Doodle.

He went up to the cage and opened the door. Otto untied her hands and took the gag from her mouth.

"We have to hurry," she said. "Those weasels are stealing from the crowd right now!"

Otto and Olivia hurried out of the tent, but Ducky Doodle stayed behind.

He went up to one of the monsters. It stared right at him. Doodle was scared, but he offered the monster an orange.

Suddenly, the curtain rose. Lights
flared in Doodle's face. He was onstage!

A scream of fright escaped from the
crowd when they saw the monsters.

"Ladies and gentlemen," said Doctor
Ocular, "this first monster…"

When they saw Ducky Doodle,
everyone began to laugh.

"What are you doing here? Get off at once!" ordered Doctor Ocular.

"No," cried Doodle. "You promised to let me feed the monsters!"

He tossed an orange at one of the monsters. It bounced off.

The crowd laughed even louder.

Doodle tossed another one. It knocked open the door of the cage.

The monster flew out and whizzed
around the tent!

The crowd screamed.

"Stop this! You're ruining the show!"
yelled Doctor Ocular.

People jumped out of their seats.

The monster circled the stage, growing smaller and smaller, until it collapsed at Doodle's feet.

"It's only a balloon!" he cried. Doctor Ocular ran off.

"And you're a fake!" shouted Doodle. He was so angry he opened all the cages, and the rest of the monsters flew out. "A fake! A fake! A fake!"

Meanwhile, Uncle Tooth, Otto, and Olivia ran after Jiminy and Biminy.

Ducky Doodle saw the weasels heading for the door. He hurled some oranges at them. They slipped on the oranges and crashed into each other. Then Uncle Tooth ran up and clamped a pair of handcuffs on their greedy little paws.

"Where's Doctor Ocular?" asked Olivia.

"There he is," cried Otto, pointing to the Floating Laboratory. "He's getting away!"

Ducky Doodle came over carrying the carpetbag filled with ticket money. "He forgot this," he said.

"Doodle!" cried Uncle Tooth. "You have saved the day!"

Later that night, Uncle Tooth sat with Ducky Doodle outside the circus tent.

"I'm so stupid," said Ducky Doodle. "I couldn't even tell that Doctor Ocular was lying to me."

"You are trusting," said Uncle Tooth. "And you must learn who is trustworthy and who is not. You are also very brave."

"But the monsters were fake."

"You didn't know that. You had to be brave to find out they weren't real. And your bravery helped catch the crooks."

"I suppose," said Ducky Doodle.

"Such bravery should be rewarded," said Uncle Tooth. "How would you like to feed some *real* sea creatures tomorrow?"

"Promise?" said Doodle.

"I promise," said Uncle Tooth.

The next morning, Otto, Olivia, Auntie Hick, and Ducky Doodle were out at sea in Uncle Tooth's boat. It was a fine, windy day. The gulls swooped in the sky above.

Uncle Tooth held Ducky Doodle as he sat on the bowsprit. Doodle tossed fish to a family of sea lions.

"Uncle Tooth," Ducky Doodle asked, "do you think I will ever see a real sea monster?"

"I wouldn't be surprised," said Uncle Tooth. "And when you do, will you promise to tell me all about it?"

"I promise!" said Ducky Doodle.